# Peppa Pig™

# George and the Noisy Baby

Peppa and George's family are having
a sleepover at Cousin Chloe's house.

Mummy Pig and Daddy Pig are
looking forward to an early night.
They've had a long journey.

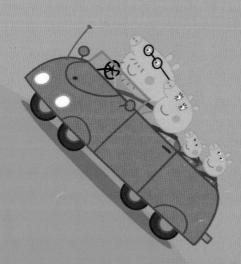

"Hello!" cries Cousin Chloe.
"Hello!" shouts Aunty Pig.
"Hello!" booms Uncle Pig.

Everyone makes a lot of noise in Cousin Chloe's house. They are a very noisy family.

"First, we'll put Baby Alexander to bed," says Aunty Pig. "This is his bedroom."

Aunty Pig turns up Baby Alexander's
musical mobile.
"Alexander likes noise," she explains.
"It sends him to sleep."

Peppa and George are staying
in Cousin Chloe's bedroom.
They are very excited.
"Night, night!" snorts Peppa.

Soon everyone is tucked up
in their beds, asleep.

"**Waaahh!**" Baby Alexander is awake.
Everyone is awake.

Uncle Pig tries
vacuuming.

Vroom!
Vroom!

Aunty Pig tries playing the trumpet.
"Noise is the best way to
get Baby Alexander
to sleep," she says.

Daddy Pig has a quieter idea to try.

"When George was a baby we used to put him in his pram and wheel him round the house," he says. "That always sent him to sleep."

Daddy Pig pushes Baby Alexander in his pram. He only has to go round the house fifty times.

"Good!" he puffs at last. "Baby Alexander is asleep."

Daddy Pig and Baby Alexander are ready to come inside. Aunty Pig switches the alarm back on.

Yawn!

"George!" cries Daddy Pig. "What are you doing up?"
"Yawn!" yawns George. "Noisy!"

Snuffle
Snuffle

Daddy Pig takes George and
Baby Alexander back up to bed.
He is about to turn the light
off when . . .

**"Waaahhhh!"**

"Uh oh!" gasps George. Baby Alexander is awake again. It is very noisy.

Daddy Pig decides to drive Baby Alexander around in the car. "Don't forget to turn off the alarm!" shouts Aunty Pig.

Daddy Pig forgets to turn off the alarm. The noisy house wakes everyone up. Miss Rabbit zooms across in her rescue helicopter.

"Is everyone all right down there?" yells Miss Rabbit.
"Yes, thank you!" bellows Uncle Pig.

The alarm has worked. Baby Alexander is fast asleep.
"And it's all down to my noisy daddy!" giggles Peppa.

# Collect these other great Peppa Pig stories

 Daddy Pig's Office

 Dentist Trip

 The Story of Prince George

 George's First Day at Playgroup

 George's New Dinosaur

 Peppa Goes Camping

 Peppa Goes Skiing

 Peppa Goes Swimming

 Peppa's First Sleepover

 Fun at the Fair

 Peppa Meets The Queen

 Peppa Pig's Family Computer

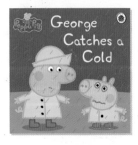 George Catches a Cold

 Peppa's First Glasses

 Peppa Plays Football

 George's Balloon